Oh Romeow, Where Art Thou?

Written by
Judith Friedlander

&

Illustrated by
Jessie Friedlander

Dedicated to my wonderful
grandchildren:
Phillip, Jessie, Paul,
and Alvaro

I would like to acknowledge my son,
Daniel Friedlander, for his invaluable
help in producing this book.

It rained and rained for 40 days and in that time, he felt hopelessly lost. He was cold, drenched and shivering.

What had happened to bring him to this place? Where was the family that loved him so much? Where was his sweet life of cushy chairs, cool water, crunchy food, and brushings that thrilled and tickled him?

They had called him Romeow, for he was a lover by nature, purring and delighting them with quirky positions that made him so adorable. They had rescued him once when he was found in the streets and taken to a pound.

"So why haven't they rescued me by now?"

He thought long and hard about what had brought him to this dismal place. What was he going to do?

He remembered how cold and dreary it was outside and his family's faces wrinkled with frowns. The wood burned day and night. The whole family sighing:

...ahh...ohh...hmm...

Then one day there was much hustle and bustle. Suitcases were pulled, lights turned off; embers extinguished and Romeow's bowl placed in the pantry, filled to the brim with food. A big jug filled with water gurgled.

The kitchen door was closed and so was his little swinging door through which he used to climb into the cozy house.

The van sped off and he had a sinking feeling that he was going to be alone for a long time. At first it was just okay, plenty of food and fresh ice-cold water. For days he darted in and out through his tiny swinging door.

He thought, "Oh well, surely, they'll return, and life will go on as usual."

Then one very rainy and windy afternoon he left the
house to hunt down some fresh food. The food in the
bowl was just getting stale.

He ran here and there, in the house, through the
fields, under the neighbors' homes, around the corner
and down to the river and onto a barge.

Nothing had caught his eye. There were no critters
to hunt down; they were just too cold to come out of
hiding. So Romeow decided to return home, only to
find that his entrance was blocked by a fallen branch.

After trying to get into the house through every opening he had tried before, he felt tired and returned to the barge for a much needed nap.

Romeow woke up startled - he was confused and very dizzy. He realized that the barge had gone down river while he was asleep, and was now under an unfamiliar bridge.

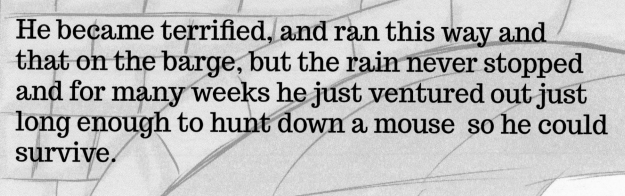

He became terrified, and ran this way and that on the barge, but the rain never stopped and for many weeks he just ventured out just long enough to hunt down a mouse so he could survive.

He tried to figure out how his family was going to rescue him. He remembered how they came to adopt him the first time. Was that possible again?

Now that the rain had stopped, he decided that he would walk the streets in search of some help. He still had a purple collar with a bell, but unfortunately the name tag and phone number had fallen off and sadly the little bell on the purple collar always scared away the birds. He hit the streets and began the walk that would possibly lead him home again.

After wandering for hours Romeow met a small boy. The boy hesitated to come near him, maybe he was taught not to get too near animals he did not know. Romeow purred and acted friendly. The boy pet him a little, but after a short time he went away.

On the next street he ran into a group of boys playing marbles, and at the sight of Romeow they decided it would be more fun to throw the marbles at him instead.

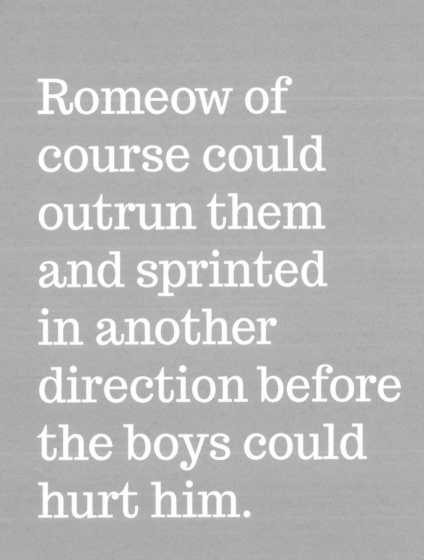

Romeow of course could outrun them and sprinted in another direction before the boys could hurt him.

It was getting late and dark, and he saw that this day was not successful. However, he would not give up. He was hopeful.

Romeow decided to settle down on the back porch of a very old house. It was somewhat rickety and in need of repair;

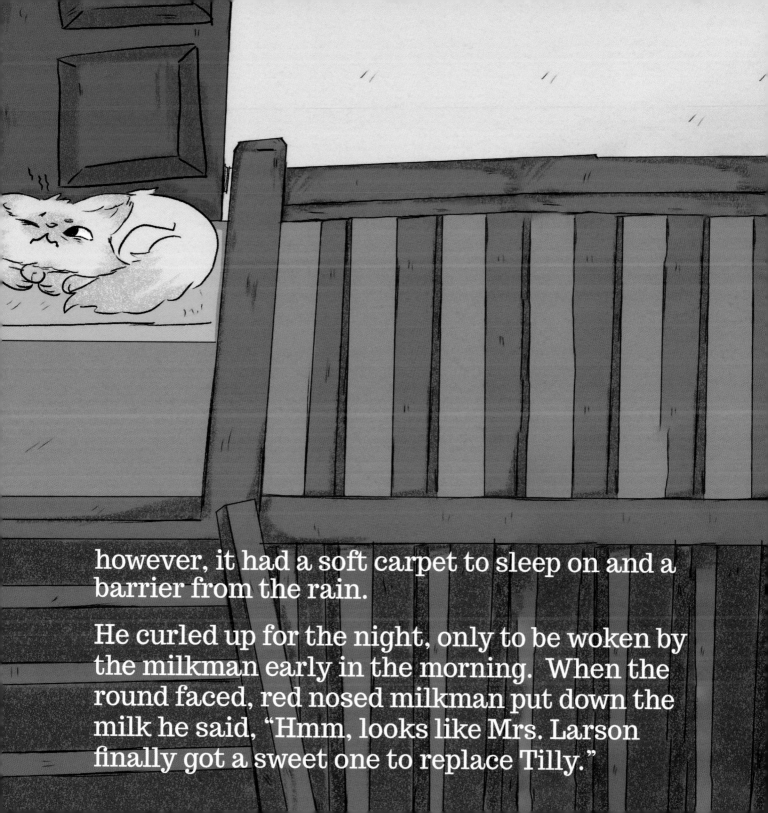

however, it had a soft carpet to sleep on and a barrier from the rain.

He curled up for the night, only to be woken by the milkman early in the morning. When the round faced, red nosed milkman put down the milk he said, "Hmm, looks like Mrs. Larson finally got a sweet one to replace Tilly."

After a time, an elderly woman appeared at the door and when she saw Romeow, a tear welled from her eye. Before long she appeared with a flowered dish full of warm milk on one side and tuna fish on the other.

'Oh,' Romeow thought, 'not crunchy, but soooo delicious.'

When he finished eating, he felt so grateful, and looked up at her and rubbed his head against her flannel pajamas. He purred and cocked his head to one side, sending her all his charm.

She smiled back, and opened the door to her house to let him in. He found many comfortable chairs covered in furry soft material. It was of course his duty to check the house inside and out, and that is what he did.

Again, he heard those familiar sighs he had heard from his other family, coming from Mrs. Larson.

Sigh, sigh, sigh...

"What am I to do?"

This frightened him a bit, but she did not go away.

Mrs. Larson had instantly fallen in love, and this new guest in her home lifted the pain from her heart.

She decided that she could not keep the new cat until she had at least tried to find his previous owners. She made posters and hung them on posts and bulletin boards in the neighborhood. She had no way of knowing that Romeow had come such a long, long way.

Weeks passed and no one called. Slowly Romeow became very attached and comfortable in Mrs. Larson's home. Mrs. Larson secretly hoped no one would ever call, for now she was in love with Romeow.

'Hmm,' Romeow thought, 'my family did not rescue me, but Mrs. Larson has adopted me, and I love my new home and Mrs. Larson just as much. I sure hope she doesn't go away when the weather gets bad.'

The End

Notes:

Questions for Discussion:

1. What could you do to prevent the loss of your animal?

2. What would you do to find your pet?

3. What do cats find more important, their homes or their masters?

4. How would you end the story?

5. Make your own illustrations for this story.

6. What do you think Mrs. Larson named the cat?

7. Do you think the family that lost the cat tried to look for him?

About the Author

Judith Friedlander is a graduate of Brooklyn School of Nursing where she became an RN, the Bank Street College of Education where she earned a degree in School Administration, and the Parson's School of Design where she studied photography, printmaking and illustration. Judith is interested in keeping the arts alive in our school systems and spent most of her professional life as a high school principal in the United States and overseas.

Judith grew up on the East Coast of the United States and has lived in the Bahamas, Venezuela, Germany, and Costa Rica. It was in Costa Rica that her lifelong love of art blossomed.

About the Illustrator

Jessie Friedlander was born in Costa Rica where her love of art had its start. Her work is in traditional and digital media, juxtaposing fantasy, and animals with a humorous slant. Later on she moved to California with her family where she had the opportunity to experience and learn many different forms of art. After high school, Jessie is looking forward to attending an art school to fully develop her career in art.